NAPER SCHOOL
L. D. RESOURCE

W9-ABD-523

LITTLE
CHIEF

Story and pictures by
SYD HOFF

A Harper Trophy Book

Harper & Row, Publishers

I Can Read Book is a registered trademark of
Harper & Row, Publishers, Inc.

LITTLE CHIEF

Copyright © 1961 by Syd Hoff

All rights reserved. Printed in the United States of America. No part of this book may be used or reproduced in any manner whatsoever without written permission except in the case of brief quotations embodied in critical articles and reviews. For information address Harper & Row Junior Books, 10 East 53rd Street, New York, N.Y. 10022.

LC Number: 61-12098
ISBN 0-06-022501-7
ISBN 0-06-444135-0 (pbk.)
First Harper Trophy edition, 1990.

LITTLE
CHIEF

Once there were fifty tents

in a green valley.

Little Chief lived

in one of the tents.

He was an Indian boy.

6

The Indians were going hunting.

"May I go?" said Little Chief.

"No," said his father.

"Stay here and help your mother."

8

Little Chief helped his mother

sweep out the tent.

He helped her husk the corn.

He helped hang out the wash.

11

At last the work was done.

"Now you may go and play,"

said Little Chief's mother.

"Good," said Little Chief.

"I will play hunter."

13

He went into the woods.

Little Chief saw a fox.

"May I have your coat of fur?"

he asked.

"If you can catch me," said the fox.

And he ran away.

Little Chief saw a bear.

"May I have your coat of fur?"

he asked.

17

"I should say not," said the bear.

"What would I wear?"

He chased Little Chief away.

18

Little Chief saw a buffalo.

"May I have your coat of fur?"

asked Little Chief.

19

"Take it," said the buffalo.

"I am lost.

I do not care what happens to me."

"Don't be scared,"

said Little Chief.

"I am not a real hunter.

I am only playing.

Come, I will help you

find your herd."

21

They walked and walked.

"There they are," said Little Chief.

"There is your herd."

"Thank you," said the buffalo.

"I am very glad we met."

"I am, too," said Little Chief.

23

Little Chief sat down and rested.

"I wish I had someone to play with,"

he said.

"You could play with us,"

said the prairie dogs.

"You could play with us,"

said the deer.

"You could even play with us,"

said the snakes.

"I mean children,"
said Little Chief.
"I wish I had children
to play with."

28

Just then there was a loud noise.

"What is that?" said the animals.

They ran away.

The noise got louder and louder.

Little Chief hid behind a rock.

He saw what made the noise.

It was a wagon train.

"Let's stop here," said the leader.

People got off the wagons.

"Go and play,"

they told their children.

32

The children ran across the field.

One child looked behind the rock.

"See what I found," he said.

"Who are you?" asked the children.

"I am an Indian,"

said Little Chief.

"I live here."

36

"Would you like to play with us?"

asked the children.

"Yes," said Little Chief.

The children showed Little Chief

how they played.

They showed him how to play tag.

They showed him how to play leap frog.

They showed Little Chief

all the games they knew.

"What can Indians do?"

asked the children.

"They can call birds,"

said Little Chief.

He called and the birds came to him.

"They can walk without making noise,"
said Little Chief.

He walked and there wasn't a sound.

"What else can Indians do?"
said the children.
"They can do a rain dance,"
said Little Chief.

45

"Good!" said the children.

"Show us!"

Little Chief started to dance.

He waved his hands
and jumped up and down.

"It isn't raining yet,"

said the children.

49

Little Chief waved and jumped harder.

"The sun is still shining,"

said the children.

Little Chief waved and jumped
harder and harder and harder.

The children waved and jumped, too.

But it did not rain.

"Children, come back to the wagons,"
called the leader.

"Good-bye," said the children.

"It would have rained soon,"

said Little Chief.

The children ran back

across the field.

"Look out for the buffalo,"

cried Little Chief.

The buffalo ran toward the children.

"We must save them!"

said the people.

"I will save them!"

said Little Chief.

He ran in front of the children.

"It is my friend Little Chief,"
said one of the buffalo.
The herd ran the other way.

61

All the people thanked Little Chief.

"We will stay here

in the green valley," they said.

"I am glad," said Little Chief.

"We will be good friends."